This abridged edition first published in 1985 by
Deans International Publishing
52–54 Southwark Street, London SE1 1UA
A division of The Hamlyn Publishing Group Limited
London · New York · Sydney · Toronto

Text and illustrations this edition
Copyright © Deans International Publishing,
a division of The Hamlyn Publishing Group Limited, 1985

ISBN 0 603 00342 7

Printed and Bound by Purnell and Sons (Book Production) Ltd.,
Paulton,
Bristol.
Member of BPCC plc

illustrated by Harry Bishop

Illustrated Classics

AROUND THE WORLD
— IN —
EIGHTY DAYS

Jules Verne

Phileas Fogg's New Servant

Mr Phileas Fogg was every inch an Englishman who lived, in 1872, at No. 7, Savile Row, Burlington Gardens, the house in which Sheridan died in 1814. He was one of the most noticeable members of the Reform Club, though he seemed always to avoid attracting attention; an enigmatical personage, about whom little was known, except that he was an undoubtedly rich and polished man of the world. He was the least communicative of men and few knew how he had come by his money. Phileas Fogg was a member of the Reform, and that was all.

The way in which he got admission to this exclusive club was simple enough. He was recommended by the Barings, with whom he had an open credit. His cheques were regularly paid at sight from his current account, which was always flush.

Mr Fogg was not lavish, nor, on the contrary, avaricious; for whenever he knew that money was needed for a noble, useful, or benevolent purpose he supplied it quietly and sometimes anonymously.

His sole pastimes were reading the papers and playing whist. He lived alone in his house in Savile Row, where a single domestic sufficed to serve him. He breakfasted and dined at the club, at hours mathematically fixed, in the same room, at the same table, never taking his meals with other members, and went home at exactly midnight.

The mansion in Savile Row, though not sumptuous, was exceedingly comfortable. The habits of its occupant were such as to demand but little from the sole domestic, but Phileas Fogg required him to be almost superhumanly prompt and regular.

On this very 2nd of October he had dismissed James Forster, because that luckless youth had brought him shaving-water at eighty-four degrees Fahrenheit instead of eighty-six; and he was awaiting his successor, who was due at the house between eleven and half-past.

Phileas Fogg was seated squarely in his armchair, his feet close together like those of a grenadier on parade, his hands resting on his knees, his body straight, his head erect; he was steadily watching a complicated clock which indicated the hours, the minutes, the seconds, the days, the months, and the years. At exactly half-past eleven Mr Fogg would, according to his daily habit, quit Savile Row, and repair to the Reform.

A rap at this moment sounded on the door of the cosy apartment where Phileas Fogg was seated, and James Forster, the dismissed servant, appeared.

"This is the new servant," said he.

A young man of thirty advanced and bowed.

"You are a Frenchman, I believe," asked Phileas Fogg, "and your name is John?"

"Jean, if monsieur pleases," replied the newcomer, "Jean Passepartout, a surname which has clung to me because I have a natural aptness for going out of one business into another. I believe I'm honest, monsieur, but, to be outspoken, I've had several trades."

"You are well recommended to me; I hear a good report of you. You know my conditions?" asked Mr Fogg.

"Yes, monsieur."

"Good. What time is it?"

"Twenty-two minutes after eleven," returned Passepartout, drawing an enormous silver watch from the depths of his pocket.

"You are too slow," said Mr Fogg.

"Pardon me, monsieur, it is impossible—"

"You are four minutes too slow. No matter; it's enough to mention the error. Now from this moment, twenty-six minutes after eleven, a.m., this Wednesday, October 2nd, you are in my service."

Phileas Fogg got up, took his hat in his left hand, put it on his head with an automatic motion, and went off without a word.

Passepartout heard the street door shut once; it was his new master going out. He heard it shut again; it was his predecessor, James Forster, departing in his turn. Passepartout remained alone in the house in Savile Row.

Passepartout Finds His Ideal Master

During his brief interview with Mr Fogg, Passepartout had been carefully observing him. He appeared to be a man about forty years of age, with fine, handsome features and a tall, well-shaped figure; his hair and whiskers were light, his forehead compact and unwrinkled, his face rather pale, his teeth magnificent.

As for Passepartout, he was a true Parisian of Paris. Since he had abandoned his own country for England, taking service as a valet, he had in vain searched for a master after his own heart. Passepartout was an honest fellow, with a pleasant face, lips a trifle protruding, soft-mannered and serviceable, with a good round head, such as one likes to see on the shoulders of a friend. His eyes were blue, his complexion rubicund, his figure almost portly and well-built, his body muscular, and his physical powers fully developed by the exercises of his younger days. His brown hair was somewhat tumbled.

It would be rash to predict how Passepartout's lively nature would agree with Mr Fogg. It was impossible to tell whether the new servant would turn out as absolutely methodical as his master required; experience alone could solve the question. Passepartout had been a sort of vagrant in his early years, and now yearned for repose; but so far he had failed to find it, though he had already served in ten English houses. But he could not take root in any of these.

At half-past eleven, then, Passepartout found himself alone in the house in Savile Row. He began his inspection without delay, scouring it from cellar

to garret. So clean, well-arranged, solemn a mansion pleased him; it seemed to him like a snail's shell, lighted and warmed by gas, which sufficed for both these purposes. When Passepartout reached the second storey he recognized at once the room which he was to inhabit, and he was well satisfied with it. Electric bells and speaking-tubes afforded communication with the lower stories; while on the mantel stood an electric clock, precisely like that in Mr Fogg's bedchamber, both beating the same second at the same instant.

"That's good, that'll do," said Passepartout to himself.

He suddenly observed, hung over the clock, a card, which, upon inspection, proved to be a programme of the daily routine of the house. It comprised all that was required of the servant, from eight in the morning, exactly at which hour Phileas Fogg rose, till half-past eleven, when he left the house for the Reform Club—all the details of service, the tea and toast at twenty-three minutes past eight, the shaving-water at thirty-seven minutes past nine, and the toilet at twenty minutes before ten. Everything was regulated and foreseen that was to be done from half-past eleven a.m. till midnight, the hour at which the methodical gentleman retired.

Mr Fogg's wardrobe was amply supplied and in the best taste. Each pair of trousers, coat, and vest bore a number, indicating the time of year and season at which they were in turn to be laid out for wearing; and the same system was applied to the master's shoes. In short, the house in Savile Row, which must have been a very temple of disorder and unrest under the illustrious but dissipated Sheridan, was cosiness, comfort, and method idealized. There was no study, nor were there books, which would have been quite useless to Mr Fogg; for at the Reform two libraries, one of general literature and the other of law and politics, were at his service. A moderate-sized safe stood in his bedroom, constructed so as to defy fire as well as burglars; but Passepartout found neither arms nor hunting weapons anywhere; everything betrayed the most tranquil and peaceable habits.

Having scrutinized the house from top to bottom, he rubbed his hands, a broad smile overspread his features, and he said joyfully, "This is just what I wanted! Ah, we shall get on together, Mr Fogg and I! What a domestic and regular gentleman, a real machine! Well, I don't mind serving a machine."

A Wager

Mr Fogg had been at the Reform Club for most of the day, where he had been perusing the daily papers. After dining, he returned to the reading-room and at precisely twenty minutes before six, he sat down to the *Pall Mall*.

Half an hour later, several members of the Reform came in and drew up to the fireplace, where a coal fire was steadily burning. They were Mr Fogg's usual partners at whist: Andrew Stuart, an engineer; John Sullivan and Samuel Fallentin, bankers; Thomas Flanagan, a brewer; and Gauthier Ralph, one of the directors of the Bank of England—all rich and highly respectable personages, even in a club which comprises the princes of English trade and finance.

"Well, Ralph," said Thomas Flanagan, "what about that robbery?"

"Oh," replied Stuart, "the bank will lose the money."

"On the contrary," broke in Ralph, "I hope we may put our hands on the robber. Skilful detectives have been sent to all the principal ports of America

and the continent, and he'll be a clever fellow if he slips through their fingers.''

''But have you got the robber's description?'' asked Stuart.

''In the first place, he is no robber at all,'' returned Ralph, positively.

''What? A fellow who makes off with fifty-five thousand pounds no robber?''

''No.''

''Perhaps he's a manufacturer, then.''

''The *Daily Telegraph*, however, says that he is a gentleman.''

It was Phileas Fogg, whose head now emerged from behind his newspapers, who made this remark. He bowed to his friends, and entered into the conversation. The affair which formed its subject, and which was town talk, had occurred three days before at the Bank of England. A package of banknotes, to the value of fifty-five thousand pounds, had been taken from the principal cashier's table.

As soon as the robbery was discovered, picked detectives hastened off to Liverpool, Glasgow, Havre, Suez, Brindisi, New York, and other ports, inspired by the proffered reward of two thousand pounds, and five per cent on the sum that might be recovered. Detectives were also charged with narrowly watching those who arrived at or left London by rail, and a judicial examination was at once entered upon.

As they placed themselves at the whist table, the gentlemen continued to argue the matter. Stuart and Flanagan played together, while Phileas Fogg had Fallentin for his partner. As the game proceeded the conversation ceased, excepting between the rubbers, when it revived again.

"I maintain," said Stuart, "that the chances are in favour of the thief, who must be a shrewd fellow."

"Well, but where can he fly to?" said Ralph. "No country is safe for him."

"Pshaw!"

"Where could he go, then?"

"Oh, I don't know that. The world is big enough."

"It was once," said Phileas Fogg, in a low tone. "Cut, sir," he added, handing the cards to Thomas Flanagan.

The discussion fell during the rubber, after which Stuart took up its thread.

"What do you mean by 'once'? Has the world grown smaller?"

"Certainly," returned Ralph. "I agree with Mr Fogg. The world *has* grown smaller, since a man can now go round it ten times more quickly than a hundred years ago. And that is why the search for this thief will be more likely to succeed."

"And also why the thief can get away more easily."

"Be so good as to play, Mr Stuart," said Phileas Fogg.

But the incredulous Stuart was not convinced, and when the hand was finished, said eagerly: "You have a strange way, Ralph, of proving that the world has grown smaller. So, because you can go round it in three months—"

"In eighty days," interrupted Phileas Fogg.

"That is true, gentlemen," added John Sullivan; "only eighty days, now that the section between Rothal and Allahabad, on the Great Indian Peninsula Railway, has been opened. Here is the estimate made by the *Daily Telegraph*:

From London to Suez via Mont Cenis and Brindisi, by rail and steamboats	7 days
From Suez to Bombay, by steamer	13 ,,
From Bombay to Calcutta, by rail	3 ,,
From Calcutta to Hong Kong, by steamer	13 ,,
From Hong Kong to Yokohama (Japan), by steamer	6 ,,
From Yokohama to San Francisco, by steamer	22 ,,
From San Francisco to New York, by rail	7 ,,
From New York to London, by steamer and rail	9 ,,
Total	80 days."

"Yes, in eighty days!" exclaimed Stuart, who in his excitement made a false deal. "But that doesn't take into account bad weather, contrary winds, shipwrecks, railway accidents, and so on."

"All included," returned Phileas Fogg.

"But suppose the Hindoos or Indians pull up the rails," replied Stuart; "suppose they stop the trains, pillage the luggage vans, and scalp the passengers?"

"All included," calmly retorted Fogg; adding, as he threw down the cards, "Two trumps."

Stuart, whose turn it was to deal, gathered them up, and went on: "You are right, theoretically, Mr Fogg, but practically—"

"Practically also, Mr Stuart."

"I'd like to see you do it in eighty days."

"It depends on you. Shall we go?"

"Heaven preserve me! But I would wager four thousand pounds that such a journey, made under these conditions, is impossible."

"Quite possible, on the contrary," returned Mr Fogg.

"Well, make it, then!"

"The journey round the world in eighty days?"

"Yes."

"I should like nothing better."

"When?"

"At once. Only it will be at your expense."

"It's absurd!" cried Stuart, who was beginning to be annoyed at the persistency of his friend. "Come, let's get on with the game."

"Deal over again, then," said Phileas Fogg.

Stuart took up the pack with a feverish hand.

"Well, Mr Fogg," said he, "it shall be so: I will wager the four thousand on it."

"Calm yourself, my dear Stuart," said Fallentin. "It's only a joke."

"When I say I'll wager," returned Stuart, "I mean it."

"All right," said Mr Fogg; and turning to the others he continued: "I have a deposit of twenty thousand at Baring's, which I will willingly risk upon it."

"Twenty thousand pounds!" cried Sullivan. "Twenty thousand pounds, which you would lose by a single accidental delay!"

"The unforeseen does not exist," quietly replied Phileas Fogg.

"But, Mr Fogg, eighty days are only the estimate of the least possible time in which the journey can be made."

"A well-used minimum suffices for everything."

"But, in order not to exceed it, you must jump mathematically from the trains upon the steamers, and from the steamers upon the trains again."

"I will jump—mathematically."

"You are joking."

"A true Englishman doesn't joke when he is talking about so serious a thing as a wager," replied Phileas Fogg solemnly. "I will bet twenty thousand pounds against anyone who wishes that I will make the tour of the world in eighty days or less; in nineteen hundred and twenty hours, or a hundred and fifteen thousand two hundred minutes. Do you accept?"

"We accept," replied Messrs Stuart, Fallentin, Sullivan, Flanagan, and Ralph, after consulting each other.

"Good," said Mr Fogg. "The train leaves for Dover at a quarter before nine. I will take it."

"This very evening?" asked Stuart.

"This very evening," returned Phileas Fogg. He took out and consulted a pocket almanac, and added, "As today is Wednesday, the second of October, I shall be due in London, in this very room of the Reform Club, on Saturday, the twenty-first of December, at a quarter before 9 p.m.; or else the twenty thousand pounds, now deposited in my name at Baring's, will belong to you, in fact and in right, gentlemen. Here is a cheque for the amount."

A memorandum of the wager was at once drawn up and signed by the six parties, during which Phileas Fogg preserved a stoical composure. He certainly did not bet to win, and had only staked the twenty thousand pounds, half of his fortune, because he foresaw that he might have to expend the other half to carry out this difficult, not to say unattainable, project. As for his antagonists, they seemed much agitated, not so much by the value of their stake, as because they had some scruples about betting under conditions so difficult to their friend.

The clock struck seven, and the party offered to suspend the game so that Mr Fogg might make his preparations for departure.

"I am quite ready now," was his tranquil response. "Diamonds are trumps: be so good as to play, gentlemen."

Passepartout is Stupefied

Having won twenty guineas at whist, and taken leave of his friends, Phileas Fogg, at twenty-five minutes past seven, left the Reform Club.

Passepartout, who had conscientiously studied the programme of his duties, was more than surprised to see his master guilty of the inexactness of appearing at this unaccustomed hour; for, according to rule, he was not due in Savile Row until precisely midnight.

Mr Fogg repaired to his bedroom, and called out, "Passepartout!"

Passepartout did not reply. It could not be he who had called; it was not the right hour.

"Passepartout!" repeated Mr Fogg, without raising his voice.

Passepartout made his appearance.

"I've called you twice," observed his master.

"But it is not midnight," responded the other, showing his watch.

"I know it; I don't blame you. We start for Dover and Calais in ten minutes."

A puzzled grin overspread Passepartout's round face; clearly he had not comprehended his master.

"Monsieur is going to leave home?"

"Yes," returned Phileas Fogg. "We are going round the world."

Passepartout opened wide his eyes, raised his eyebrows, held up his hands, and seemed about to collapse, so overcome was he with stupefied astonishment.

"Round the world!" he murmured.

"In eighty days," responded Mr Fogg. "So we haven't a moment to lose."

"But the trunks," gasped Passepartout, unconsciously swaying his head from right to left.

"We'll have no trunks; only a carpet-bag, with two shirts and three pairs of stockings for me, and the same for you. We'll buy our clothes on the way. Bring down my mackintosh and travelling cloak, and some stout shoes, though we shall do little walking. Make haste!"

Passepartout tried to reply, but could not. He went out, mounted to his own room, fell into a chair, and muttered: "That's good, that is! And I, who wanted to remain quiet!"

By eight o'clock Passepartout had packed the modest carpet-bag, containing the wardrobe of his master and himself; then, still troubled in mind, he carefully shut the door of his room, and descended to Mr Fogg.

Mr Fogg was quite ready. Under his arm might have been observed a red-bound copy of *Bradshaw's Continental Railway Steam Transit and General Guide*, with its timetables showing the arrival and departure of steamers and railways. He took the carpet-bag, opened it, and slipped into it a goodly roll of Bank of England notes, which would pass wherever he might go.

"You have forgotten nothing?" asked he.

"Nothing, monsieur."

"My mackintosh and cloak?"

"Here they are."

"Good. Take this carpet-bag," handing it to Passepartout. "Take good care of it, for there are twenty thousand pounds in it."

Passepartout nearly dropped the bag, as if the twenty thousand pounds were in gold, and weighed him down.

Master and man then descended, the street-door was double locked, and at the end of Savile Row they took a cab and drove rapidly to Charing Cross. The cab stopped before the railway station at twenty minutes past eight. Passepartout jumped off the box and followed his master, who, after paying the cabman, was about to enter the station, when a poor beggar-woman, with a child in her arms, her naked feet smeared with mud, her head covered with a wretched bonnet, from which hung a tattered feather, and her shoulders shrouded in a ragged shawl, approached, and mournfully asked for alms.

Mr Fogg took out the twenty guineas he had just won at whist, and handed them to the beggar, saying, "Here, my good woman. I'm glad that I met you"; and passed on.

Passepartout had a moist sensation about the eyes; his master's action touched his susceptible heart.

Two first-class tickets for Paris having been speedily purchased, Mr Fogg was crossing the station to the train when he perceived his five friends of the Reform.

"Well, gentlemen," said he, "I'm off, you see; and if you will examine my passport when I get back, you will be able to judge whether I have accomplished the journey agreed upon."

"Oh, that would be quite unnecessary, Mr Fogg," said Ralph politely. "We will trust your word, as a gentleman of honour."

Phileas Fogg and his servant seated themselves in a first-class carriage at twenty minutes before nine; five minutes later the whistle screamed, and the train slowly glided out of the station.

The night was dark, and a fine, steady rain was falling. Phileas Fogg, snugly ensconced in his corner, did not open his lips. Passepartout, not yet recovered from his stupefaction, clung mechanically to the carpet-bag, with its enormous treasure.

Detective Fix

The Commissioner of Police was sitting in his office at nine o'clock one evening, when the following telegraphic despatch was put into his hands:

Suez to London
ROWAN, COMMISSIONER OF POLICE, SCOTLAND YARD:

    I've found the bank robber, Phileas Fogg. Send without delay warrant of arrest to Bombay.
                      Fix, *Detective.*

The effect of this despatch was instantaneous. The idea of Fogg as the polished gentleman, held at the Reform Club, disappeared to give place to the bank robber. His photograph, which was hung with those of the rest of the members at the Reform Club, was minutely examined, and it betrayed, feature by feature, the description of the robber which had been provided to the police. The mysterious habits of Phileas Fogg were recalled; his solitary ways, his sudden departure; and it seemed clear that, in undertaking a tour round the world on the pretext of a wager, he had had no other end in view than to elude the detectives and throw them off his track.

The circumstances under which this telegraphic despatch about Phileas Fogg was sent were as follows:

The steamer *Mongolia* was due at eleven o'clock

a.m. on Wednesday, the 9th of October, at Suez, and Fix was there pacing up and down the wharves waiting for its arrival. Fix was a small, slight-built personage, with a nervous, intelligent face, and bright eyes peering out from under eyebrows which he was incessantly twitching. He was one of the detectives who had been despatched from England in search of the bank robber, and he was evidently inspired by the hope of obtaining the splendid reward which would be the prize of success, and so he awaited, with a feverish impatience, the arrival of the steamer.

Little by little the scene on the quay became more animated; sailors of various nations, merchants, shipbrokers, porters, fellahs, bustled to and fro as if

the steamer were immediately expected. The weather was clear, and slightly chilly. The minarets of the town loomed above the houses in the pale rays of the sun. A jetty pier, some two thousand yards long, extended into the roadstead. A number of fishing-smacks and coasting boats, some retaining the fantastic fashion of ancient galleys, were discernible on the Red Sea.

As he passed among the busy crowd, Fix, according to habit, scrutinized the passers-by with a keen, rapid glance.

Then there sounded a succession of sharp whistles, which announced the arrival of the *Mongolia*. The porters and fellahs rushed down the quay, and a dozen boats pushed off from the shore to go and meet the steamer. Soon her gigantic hull appeared, passing along between the banks, and eleven o'clock struck as she anchored in the road. She brought an unusual number of passengers, some of whom remained on deck to scan the picturesque panorama of the town, while the greater part disembarked in the boats, and landed on the quay.

Fix took up a position, and carefully examined each face and figure which made its appearance. Presently, one of the passengers, after vigorously pushing his way through the importunate crowd of porters, came up to him and politely asked if he could point out the English consulate, at the same time showing a passport which he wished to have visaed. Fix instinctively took the passport, and with a rapid glance read the description of its bearer. An involuntary motion of surprise nearly escaped him, for the description in the passport was identical with that of the bank robber which he had received from Scotland Yard.

"Is this your passport?" asked he.

"No, it is my master's."

"And your master is—"

"He stayed on board."

"But he must go to the consulate in person, so as to establish his identity."

"Oh, is that necessary?"

"Quite indispensable."

"And where is the consulate?"

"There, on the corner of the square," said Fix, pointing to a house two hundred steps off.

"I'll go and fetch my master, who won't be much pleased to be disturbed."

The passenger bowed to Fix, and returned to the steamer.

A Visit to the Consul

The detective passed down the quay, and rapidly made his way to the consul's office, where he was at once admitted to the presence of that official.

"Consul," said he, without preamble, "I have strong reasons for believing that a man I am looking for on account of a robbery is a passenger on the *Mongolia*." And he narrated what had just passed concerning the passport.

"Well, Mr Fix," replied the consul, "I shall not be sorry to see the rascal's face; but perhaps he won't come here—that is, if he is the person you suppose him to be. A robber doesn't quite like to leave traces of his flight behind him; and besides, he is not obliged to have his passport countersigned."

"If he is as shrewd as I think he is, consul, he will come."

"To have his passport visaed?"

"Yes, and I must keep this man here until I can get a warrant to arrest him from London."

"Ah, that's your look-out. But I cannot——"

The consul did not finish his sentence, for as he spoke a knock was heard on the door, and two strangers entered, one of whom was the servant whom Fix had met on the quay. The other, who was

his master, held out his passport with the request that the consul would do him the favour to visa it. The consul took the document and carefully read it, whilst Fix observed, or rather devoured, the stranger with his eyes from a corner of the room.

The consul proceeded to sign and date the passport, after which he added his official seal. Mr Fogg paid the customary fee, coldly bowed, and went out, followed by his servant.

Mr Fogg, after leaving the consulate, repaired to the quay, gave some orders to Passepartout, went off to the *Mongolia* in a boat, and descended to his cabin. He took up his notebook, which contained the following memoranda:

"Left London, Wednesday, October 2nd, at 8.45 p.m.

"Reached Paris, Thursday, October 3rd, at 7.30 a.m.

"Left Paris, Thursday, at 8.40 a.m.

"Reached Turin by Mont Cenis, Friday, October 4th, at 6.35 a.m.

"Left Turin, Friday, at 7.20 a.m.

"Arrived at Brindisi, Saturday, October 5th, at 4 p.m.

"Sailed on the *Mongolia*, Saturday, at 5 p.m.

"Reached Suez, Wednesday, October 9th, at 11 a.m.

"Total of hours spent, $158\frac{1}{2}$: or, in days, six days and a half."

Fix Talks to Passepartout

Fix soon rejoined Passepartout, who was lounging and looking about on the quay, as if he did not feel that he, at least, was obliged not to see anything.

"Well, my friend," said the detective, coming up with him, "is your passport visaed?"

"Ah, it's you, is it, monsieur?" responded Passepartout. "Thanks, yes, the passport is all right, but we travel so fast that I seem to be journeying in a dream."

"Where is your master going?"

"Always straight ahead. He is going round the world."

"Round the world?" cried Fix.

"Yes, and in eighty days! He says it is on a wager; but, between us, I don't believe a word of it. That wouldn't be common sense. There's something else in the wind."

"Ah! Mr Fogg is a character, is he?"

"I should say he was."

"Is he rich?"

"No doubt, for he is carrying an enormous sum in brand-new banknotes with him. And he doesn't spare the money on the way, either: he has offered a large reward to the engineer of the *Mongolia* if he gets us to Bombay well in advance of time."

The effect of these replies upon the already suspicious and excited detective may be imagined.

"Is Bombay far from here?" asked Passepartout.

"Pretty far. It is ten days' voyage by sea."

Fix, now fully convinced he'd got his man, left Passepartout and hurried back to the consulate.

"Consul," said he, "I have no longer any doubt. I have spotted my man. He passes himself off as an odd stick who is going round the world in eighty days."

"But are you not mistaken?"

"I am not mistaken."

He reported in a few words the most important parts of his conversation with Passepartout.

"Well, what are you going to do?"

"Send a despatch to London for a warrant of arrest to be despatched instantly to Bombay, take passage on board the *Mongolia*, follow my rogue to India, and there, on English ground, arrest him politely, with my warrant in my hand, and my hand on his shoulder."

Having uttered these words with a cool, careless air, the detective took leave of the consul, and repaired to the telegraph office, whence he sent the despatch to the London police office. A quarter of an hour later found Fix, with a small bag in his hand, proceeding on board the *Mongolia*.

And ere many moments longer, the noble steamer at last rode out at full steam upon the waters of the Red Sea.

Passepartout Loses His Shoes

The *Mongolia* was due at Bombay on the 22nd; she arrived on the 20th. This was a gain to Phileas Fogg of two days since his departure from London, and he calmly entered the fact in the itinerary, in the column of gains.

The passengers of the *Mongolia* went ashore at half-past four p.m.; at exactly eight the train would start for Calcutta.

Mr Fogg, after bidding goodbye to some whist partners, left the steamer, gave his servant several errands to do, urged it upon him to be at the station promptly at eight, and, with his regular step, which beat to the second, like an astronomical clock, directed his steps to the passport office. As for the wonders of Bombay—its famous city hall, its splendid library, its forts and docks, its bazaars, mosques, synagogues, its Armenian churches, and the noble pagoda on Malabar Hill with its two polygonal towers—he cared not a straw to see them.

Having transacted his business at the passport office, Phileas Fogg repaired quietly to the railway station, where he ordered dinner.

Fix had gone on shore shortly after Mr Fogg, and his first destination was the headquarters of the Bombay police. He made himself known as a London detective, told his business at Bombay, and the position of affairs relative to the supposed robber, and nervously asked if a warrant had arrived from London. It had not reached the office; indeed, there had not yet been time for it to arrive. Fix was sorely disappointed, and tried to obtain an order of arrest from the director of the Bombay police. This the director refused, as the matter concerned the London office, which alone could legally deliver the warrant.

Passepartout, having purchased the usual quota of shirts and shoes, took a leisurely promenade about the streets, where crowds of people of many nationalities were celebrating a sort of religious carnival, with processions and shows.

Unhappily for his master, as well as himself, his curiosity drew him unconsciously farther off than he intended to go. He was turning his steps towards the station, when he happened to espy the splendid pagoda on Malabar Hill, and was seized with an irresistible desire to see its interior. He was quite ignorant that it is forbidden for Christians to enter

certain Indian temples and that even the faithful must not go in without first leaving their shoes outside the door. It may be said here that the wise policy of the British Government severely punishes a disregard of the practices of the native religions.

Passepartout, however, thinking no harm, went in like a simple tourist, and was soon lost in admiration of the splendid Brahmin ornamentation which everywhere met his eyes, when of a sudden he found himself sprawling on the sacred flagging. He looked up to behold three enraged priests, who forthwith fell upon him, tore off his shoes, and began to beat him with loud, savage exclamations. The agile Frenchman was soon upon his feet again, and lost no time in knocking down two of his long-gowned adversaries with his fists and a vigorous application of his toes; then, rushing out of the pagoda as fast as his legs could carry him, he soon escaped the third priest by mingling with the crowd in the street.

At five minutes before eight, Passepartout, hatless, shoeless, and having in the squabble lost his package of shirts and shoes, rushed breathlessly into the station.

Fix, who had followed Mr Fogg to the station, and saw that he was really going to leave Bombay, was there, upon the platform. He had resolved to follow the supposed robber to Calcutta, and farther, if necessary. Passepartout did not observe the detective, who stood in an obscure corner; but Fix heard him relate his adventures in a few words to Mr Fogg.

"I hope that this will not happen again," said Phileas Fogg, coldly, as he got into the train.

Poor Passepartout, quite crestfallen, followed his master without a word. Fix was on the point of entering another carriage, when an idea struck him which induced him to alter his plan.

"No, I'll stay," he muttered. "An offence has been committed on Indian soil. I've got my man."

Just then the locomotive gave a sharp screech, and the train passed out into the darkness of the night.

An Unusual Means of Transport

At half-past twelve the train stopped at Burhampoor, where Passepartout was able to purchase some Indian slippers, ornamented with false pearls, in which, with evident vanity, he proceeded to encase his feet. The travellers made a hasty breakfast and started off for Assurghur, after skirting for a little the banks of the small river Tapty, which empties into the Gulf of Cambray, near Surat.

The train stopped at eight o'clock, in the midst of a glade some fifteen miles beyond Rothal, where there were several bungalows, and workmen's cabins. The conductor, passing along the carriages, shouted, "Passengers will get out here!"

Phileas Fogg looked at Sir Francis Cromarty, his travelling companion from the *Mongolia*, for an explanation; but the general could not tell what meant a halt in the midst of this forest of dates and acacias.

Passepartout, not less surprised, rushed out and speedily returned, crying: "Monsieur, no more railway!"

"What do you mean?" asked Sir Francis.

"I mean to say that the train isn't going on."

The general at once stepped out, while Phileas Fogg calmly followed him, and they proceeded together to the conductor.

"Where are we?" asked Sir Francis.

"At the hamlet of Kholby."

"Do we stop here?"

Certainly. The railway isn't finished."

"What, not finished?"

"No. There's still a matter of fifty miles to be laid from here to Allahabad, where the line begins again."

"Yet you sell tickets from Bombay to Calcutta," retorted Sir Francis, who was growing warm.

"No doubt," replied the conductor; "but the passengers know that they must provide means of transportation for themselves from Kholby to Allahabad."

Sir Francis was furious. Passepartout would willingly have knocked the conductor down, and did not dare to look at his master.

"Sir Francis," said Mr Fogg, quietly, "we will, if you please, look about for some means of conveyance to Allahabad."

"Mr Fogg, this is a delay greatly to your disadvantage."

"No, Sir Francis; it was foreseen."

"What? You knew that the way——?"

"Not at all; but I knew that some obstacle or other would sooner or later arise on my route. Nothing, therefore, is lost. I have two days, which I have already gained, to sacrifice. A steamer leaves Calcutta for Hong Kong at noon, on the 25th. This is the 22nd, and we shall reach Calcutta in time."

There was nothing to say to so confident a response.

Mr Fogg and Sir Francis Cromarty, after searching the village from end to end, came back without finding any transport.

Happily, Passepartout found a means of conveyance—an elephant. The elephant's name was Kiouni, whose Indian owner told them it could travel rapidly for a long time. Mr Fogg resolved to hire the elephant, but the owner would not agree over the hiring price. Mr Fogg then decided to buy the animal outright, but not until the figure of two thousand pounds was reached would the Indian yield. Mr Fogg paid without hesitation, for it was necessary that he should have the elephant and start travelling without delay.

A young Parsee with an intelligent face who was an accomplished elephant driver offered his services as a guide, which Mr Fogg accepted, promising a generous reward. The elephant was duly equipped with a saddle cloth and some curiously uncomfortable howdahs. Some provisions were purchased at Kholby. Phileas Fogg offered to take Sir Francis with them, and the general gratefully accepted.

When all was ready, Sir Francis and Mr Fogg took the howdahs on either side, Passepartout got astride the saddle-cloth between them. The Parsee perched himself on the elephant's neck, and at nine o'clock they set out from the village, the animal marching off through the dense forest of palms by the shortest cut.

A Procession in the Forest

Phileas Fogg and Sir Francis Cromarty, plunged to the neck in the peculiar howdahs provided for them, were horribly jostled by the swift trotting of the elephant, spurred on as he was by the skilful Parsee; but they endured the discomfort with true British phlegm, talking little, and scarcely able to catch a glimpse of each other. Passepartout, who was mounted on the beast's back, received the direct force of each concussion as he trod along.

After two hours the guide stopped the elephant and gave him an hour for rest, during which Kiouni quenched his thirst at a neighbouring spring.

At noon the Parsee gave the signal for departure. The country soon presented a very savage aspect, vast dry plains dotted with scanty shrubs, and sown with great blocks of syenite.

The principal chain of the Vindhias was crossed by eight in the evening, and another halt was made on the northern slope, in a ruined bungalow. They had gone nearly twenty-five miles that day, and an equal distance still separated them from the station of Allahabad.

As the night was cold, the Parsee lit a fire in the bungalow with a few dry branches, and the warmth was very grateful. The provisions purchased at Kholby sufficed for supper, and the travellers ate ravenously. The conversation, beginning with a few disconnected phrases, soon gave place to loud and steady snores. Nothing occurred during the night to disturb the slumberers.

The journey was resumed at six in the morning, as the guide hoped to reach Allahabad by evening. Towards noon they passed by the village of Kallenger, on the Cani, one of the branches of the Ganges. The guide kept to the open country until Allahabad was now only twelve miles to the north-east. They stopped under a clump of bananas, the fruit of which, as healthy as bread and as succulent as cream, was amply partaken of and appreciated.

At two o'clock the guide entered a thick forest which extended several miles; he preferred now to travel under cover of the woods. They had not as yet had any unpleasant encounters, and the journey seemed on the point of being successfully accomplished, when the elephant, becoming restless, suddenly stopped. It was then four o'clock.

"What's the matter?" asked Sir Francis, putting out his head.

"I don't know officer," replied the Parsee, listening attentively to a confused murmur which came through the thick branches.

The murmur soon became more distinct; it now seemed like a distant concert of human voices accompanied by brass instruments. "A procession of Brahmins is coming this way," said the Parsee. "We must prevent their seeing us."

The guide led the elephant into a thicket, at the same time asking the travellers not to stir. He held himself ready to bestride the animal at a moment's notice, should flight become necessary.

The discordant tones of voices and instruments drew nearer. The head of the procession soon appeared beneath the trees, a hundred paces away; and the strange figures who performed the religious ceremony were easily distinguished through the branches. First came the priests with mitres on their heads, and clothed in long lace robes. They were surrounded by men, women, and children, who sang a kind of lugubrious psalm, interrupted at regular intervals by tambourines and cymbals; while behind them was drawn a car with large wheels, the spokes of which represented serpents entwined with each other. Upon the car, which was drawn by four richly caparisoned zebus, stood a hideous statue with four arms, the body coloured a dull red, with haggard eyes, dishevelled hair, protruding tongue, and lips tinted with betel. It stood upright upon the figure of a prostrate and headless giant.

Sir Francis, recognizing the statue, whispered, "The Goddess Kali, the goddess of love and death."

The Parsee made a motion to keep silence. Some Brahmins, clad in all the sumptuousness of Oriental apparel, and leading a woman who faltered at every step, followed. This woman was young, and as fair as a European. Her head and neck, shoulders, ears, arms, hands, and toes, were loaded down with jewels and gems—with bracelets, earrings and rings; while a tunic bordered with gold, and covered with a light muslin robe, betrayed the outline of her form.

The guards who followed the young woman presented a violent contrast to her, armed as they were with naked sabres hung at their waists, and long damascened pistols, and bearing a corpse on a palanquin. It was the body of an old man, gorgeously arrayed in the habiliments of a rajah, wearing, as in life, a turban embroidered with pearls, a robe of tissue of silk and gold, a scarf of cashmere sewn with diamonds, and the magnificent weapons of a Hindoo prince. Next came the musicians and the rearguard of capering fakirs, whose cries sometimes drowned the noise of the instruments; these closed the procession.

Sir Francis watched the procession with a sad countenance, and, turning to the guide, said, "A suttee."

The Parsee nodded. The procession slowly wound under the trees, and soon its last ranks disappeared in the depths of the wood. The songs gradually died away; occasionally cries were heard in the distance, until at last all was silence again.

Phileas Fogg had heard what Sir Francis said, and, as soon as the procession had disappeared, asked: "What is a 'suttee'?"

"A suttee," returned the general, "is a human sacrifice, but a voluntary one. The woman you have just seen will be burned tomorrow at the dawn of day, and, if she were not, you couldn't conceive what terrible treatment she would be obliged to submit to from her relatives."

"And the corpse?" asked Mr Fogg.

"Is that of the prince, her husband," said the guide; "an independent rajah of Bundelcund."

"Where are they taking her?" asked Sir Francis.

"To the pagoda of Pillaji, two miles from here; she will pass the night there," the Parsee informed them.

"And the sacrifice will take place—?"

"Tomorrow, at the first light of dawn."

The guide now led the elephant out of the thicket, and leaped upon his neck. Just at the moment that he was about to urge Kiouni forward with a peculiar whistle, Mr Fogg stopped him, and, turning to Sir Francis Cromarty, said, "Suppose we save this woman?"

"Save the woman, Mr Fogg?"

"I have yet twelve hours to spare; I can devote them to that."

"Why, you are a man of heart!"

"Sometimes," replied Phileas Fogg, quietly: "when I have the time."

Passepartout's Daring Feat

They all agreed that the project was a bold one, but they were all willing to risk life or liberty for the sake of the woman.

"I think we must wait till night before acting," suggested Mr Fogg.

"I think so," agreed the guide.

The worthy Indian then gave some account of the victim, who, he said, was a celebrated beauty of the Parsee race, and the daughter of a wealthy Bombay merchant. She has received a thoroughly English education in that city, and, from her manners and intelligence, would be thought European. Her name was Aouda. Left an orphan, she was married against her will to the old rajah of Bundelcund; and, knowing the fate that awaited her, she escaped, was retaken, and devoted by the rajah's relatives, who had an interest in her death, to the sacrifice from which it seemed she could not escape.

The Parsee's narrative only confirmed Mr Fogg and his companions in their generous design. It was decided that the guide should direct the elephant towards the pagoda of Pillaji, which he accordingly approached as quickly as possible. They halted, half an hour afterwards, in a copse, some five hundred feet from the pagoda, where they were well concealed; but they could hear the groans and cries of the gathering.

The Parsee, leading the others, noiselessly crept through the wood, and in ten minutes they found themselves on the banks of a small stream, whence, by the light of the rosin torches, they perceived a pyre of wood, on the top of which lay the embalmed body of the rajah, which was to be burned with his wife. The pagoda, whose minarets loomed above the trees in the deepening dusk, stood a hundred steps away. Much to the guide's disappointment, the guard of the rajah, lighted by torches, were watching at the doors and marching to and fro with naked sabres; probably the priests, too, were watching within.

The Parsee, who was now convinced that it was impossible to force an entrance to the temple, advanced no farther, but led his companions back again.

They waited till midnight; but no change took place among the guards, and it became apparent that their yielding to sleep could not be relied upon.

The hours passed, and the lighter shades now announced the approach of day, though it was not yet light. The guide led them to the rear of the glade, where they were able to observe the sleeping groups.

Meanwhile Passepartout, who had perched himself on the lower branches of a tree, was resolving an idea which had first struck him like a flash, and which was now firmly lodged in his brain.

He had commenced by saying to himself, "What folly!" and then he repeated, "Why not, after all? It's a chance—perhaps the only one!" Thinking thus, he slipped, with the suppleness of a serpent, to the lowest branches, the ends of which bent almost to the ground.

This was the moment. The slumbering multitude became animated, the tambourines sounded, songs and cries arose; the hour of the sacrifice had come.

The doors of the pagoda swung open, and a bright light escaped from its interior, in the midst of which Mr Fogg and Sir Francis espied the victim. She seemed, having shaken off a stupor of intoxication, to be striving to escape from her executioner. Sir Francis's heart throbbed; and convulsively seizing Mr Fogg's hand, found in it an open knife. Just at this moment the crowd began to move. The young woman had again fallen into a stupor caused by fumes of hemp, and passed among the fakirs, who escorted her with their wild, religious cries.

Phileas Fogg and his companions, mingling in the rear ranks of the crowd, followed; and in two minutes they reached the banks of the stream, and stopped fifty paces from the pyre, upon which still lay the rajah's corpse. In the semi-obscurity they saw the victim, quite senseless, stretched out beside her husband's body. Then a torch was brought, and the wood, soaked with oil, instantly took fire.

At this moment Sir Francis and the guide seized Phileas Fogg, who, in an instant of mad generosity, was about to rush upon the scene. But he had quickly pushed them aside, when the whole scene suddenly changed. A cry of terror arose. The whole multitude prostrated themselves, terror-stricken, on the ground.

The old rajah was not dead, then, since he rose of a sudden, like a spectre, took up his wife in his arms, and descended from the pyre in the midst of the clouds of smoke, which only heightened his ghostly appearance.

Fakirs and soldiers and priests, seized with instant terror, lay there, with their faces on the ground, not daring to lift their eyes and behold such a prodigy.

The inanimate victim was borne along by the vigorous arms which supported her, and which she did not seem in the least to burden. Mr Fogg and Sir Francis stood erect and the Parsee bowed his head.

The resuscitated rajah approached Sir Francis and Mr Fogg, and, in an abrupt tone, said, "Let us be off!"

It was Passepartout himself, who had slipped upon the pyre in the midst of the smoke, and, profiting by the still overhanging darkness, had delivered the young woman from death! It was Passepartout who, playing his part with a happy audacity, had passed through the crowd amid the general terror.

A moment after, all four of the party had disappeared in the woods, and the elephant was bearing them away at a rapid pace.

Escape Across India

The rash exploit had been accomplished; and for an hour Passepartout laughed gaily at his success. Sir Francis pressed the worthy fellow's hand, and his master said, "Well done!" which, from him, was high commendation; to which Passepartout replied that all the credit of the affair belonged to Mr Fogg.

As for the young Indian woman, she had been unconscious throughout of what was passing, and now, wrapped up in a travelling-blanket, was reposing in one of the howdahs.

The station at Allahabad was reached about ten o'clock, and the interrupted line of railway being resumed, would enable them to reach Calcutta in less than twenty-four hours.

The young woman was placed in one of the waiting-rooms of the station, whilst Passepartout was charged with purchasing for her various articles of toilet, a dress, shawl, and some furs; for which his master gave him unlimited credit.

The train was about to start from Allahabad, and Mr Fogg proceeded to pay the guide the price agreed upon for his service.

"Parsee," said he to the guide, "you have been serviceable and devoted. I have paid for your service, but not for your devotion. Would you like to have this elephant? He is yours."

The guide's eyes glistened.

"Your honour is giving me a fortune!" cried he.

"Take him, guide," returned Mr Fogg, "and I shall still be your debtor."

Soon, Phileas Fogg, Sir Francis Cromarty, and Passepartout, installed in a carriage with Aouda, who had the best seat, were whirling at full speed towards Benares. It was a run of eighty miles, and was accomplished in two hours. During the journey, the young woman fully recovered her senses. What was her astonishment to find herself in this carriage on the railway, dressed in European habiliments, and with travellers who were quite strangers to her! Her companions first set about reviving her with a little liquor, and then Sir Francis narrated to her what had passed, dwelling upon the courage with which Phileas Fogg had not hesitated to risk his life to save her, and recounting the happy sequel of the venture, the result of Passepartout's rash idea.

Aouda pathetically thanked her deliverers, rather with tears than words; her fine eyes interpreted her gratitude better than her lips. Then, as her thoughts strayed back to the scene of the sacrifice, and recalled the dangers which still menaced her, she shuddered with terror.

Phileas Fogg understood what was passing in Aouda's mind, and offered, in ordered to reassure her, to escort her to Hong Kong, where she might remain safely until the affair was hushed up—an offer which she eagerly and gratefully accepted.

At half-past twelve the train stopped at Benares, which was Sir Francis Cromarty's destination, the

troops he was rejoining being encamped some miles northward of the city. He bade adieu to Phileas Fogg, wishing him all success, and expressing the hope that he would come that way again in a less original, but more profitable, fashion. Mr Fogg lightly pressed him by the hand. The parting of Aouda, who did not forget what she owed to Sir Francis, betrayed more warmth.

The railway, on leaving Benares, passed for a while along the valley of the Ganges. Through the windows of their carriage the travellers had glimpses of the diversified landscape of Behar, with its mountains clothed in verdure, its fields of barley, wheat, and corn, its jungles peopled with green alligators, its neat villages, and its still thickly-leaved forests.

Night came on; the train passed on at full speed. Calcutta was reached at seven in the morning, and the packet left for Hong Kong at noon; so that Phileas Fogg had five hours before him.

The Arrest

The train entered the station, and Passepartout, jumping out first, was followed by Mr Fogg, who assisted his fair companion to descend. Phileas Fogg intended to proceed at once to the Hong Kong steamer, in order to get Aouda comfortably settled for the voyage. He was unwilling to leave her while they were still on dangerous ground.

Just as he was leaving the station a policeman came up to him, and said, "Mr Phileas Fogg?"

"I am he."

"Is this man your servant?" added the policeman, pointing to Passepartout.

"Yes."

"Be so good, both of you, as to follow me."

Mr Fogg betrayed no surprise whatever. The policeman was a representative of the law, and law is sacred to an Englishman. Passepartout tried to reason about the matter, but the policeman tapped him with his stick, and Mr Fogg made him a signal to obey.

"May this young lady go with us?" asked he.

"She may," replied the policeman.

Mr Fogg, Aouda, and Passepartout were conducted to a palkigari, a sort of four-wheeled carriage, drawn by two horses, in which they took their places and were driven away. No one spoke during the twenty minutes which elapsed before they reached their destination.

The carriage stopped before a modest-looking house, which, however, did not have the appearance of a private mansion. The policeman having asked

his prisoners—for so, truly, they might be called—to descend, conducted them into a room with barred windows, and said: "You will appear before Judge Obadiah at half-past eight."

He then retired and closed the door.

"Why, we are prisoners!" exclaimed Passepartout, falling into a chair.

Aouda, with an emotion she tried to conceal, said to Mr Fogg: "Sir, you must leave me to my fate! It is on my account that you receive this treatment; it is for having saved me!"

Phileas Fogg contented himself with saying that it was impossible. It was quite unlikely that he should be arrested for preventing a suttee. The complainants would not dare present themselves with such a charge. There was some mistake. Moreover, he would not in any event abandon Aouda, but would escort her to Hong Kong.

"But the steamer leaves at noon," replied Passepartout, nervously.

"We shall be on board at noon," replied his master placidly.

Appearance in Court

At half-past eight the door opened, the policeman appeared, and, requesting them to follow him, led the way to an adjoining hall. It was evidently a court-room, and a crowd of Europeans and natives already occupied the rear of the apartment.

Mr Fogg and his two companions took their places on a bench opposite the desks of the magistrate and his clerk. Immediately after, Judge Obadiah, a fat, round man, followed by the clerk, entered. He proceeded to take down a wig which was hanging on a nail, and put it hurriedly on his head.

"The first case," he said.

"Phileas Fogg?" demanded Oysterpuff, the clerk.

"I am here," replied Mr Fogg.

"Passepartout?"

"Present!" responded Passepartout.

"Good," said the judge. "You have been looked for, prisoners, for two days on the trains from Bombay."

"But of what are we accused?" asked Passepartout, impatiently.

"You are about to be informed."

"I am an English subject, sir," said Mr Fogg, "and I have a right—"

"Have you been ill-treated?"

"Not at all."

"Very well; let the complainants come in."

A door was swung open by order of the judge and three Indian priests entered.

The priests took their places in front of the judge, and the clerk proceeded to read in a loud voice a complaint of sacrilege against Phileas Fogg and his servant, who were accused of having violated a place held consecrated by the Brahmin religion, the pagoda of Malabar Hill at Bombay.

"You hear the charge?" asked the judge.

"Yes, sir," replied Mr Fogg, consulting his watch, "and I admit it."

"And as proof," added the clerk, "here are the desecrator's very shoes, which he left behind him."

"My shoes!" cried Passepartout.

Fix, the detective, had foreseen the advantage which Passepartout's escapade gave him, and, delaying his departure for twelve hours, had consulted the priests of Malabar Hill. Knowing that the English authorities dealt very severely with this kind of misdemeanour, he promised them a goodly sum in damages, and sent them forward to Calcutta by the next train.

Owing to the delay caused by the rescue of the young widow, Fix and the priests reached the Indian capital before Mr Fogg and his servant.

"Inasmuch," resumed the judge, "as the English law protects equally and sternly the religions of the Indian people, and as the man Passepartout has admitted that he violated the sacred pagoda of Malabar Hill, at Bombay, on the 20th October, I

condemn the said Passepartout to imprisonment for fifteen days and a fine of three hundred pounds."

"Three hundred pounds!" cried Passepartout, startled at the largeness of the sum.

"Silence!" shouted the constable.

"And inasmuch," continued the judge, "as it is not proved that the act was not done by the connivance of the master with the servant, and as the master in any case must be held responsible for the acts of his paid servant, I condemn Phileas Fogg to a week's imprisonment and a fine of one hundred and fifty pounds."

Fix rubbed his hands softly with satisfaction; if Phileas Fogg could be detained in Calcutta a week, it would be more than time for the warrant to arrive. Passepartout was stupefied. This sentence ruined his master. A wager of twenty thousand pounds lost, because he, like a precious fool, had gone into that abominable pagoda!

Phileas Fogg, self-composed as if the judgement did not in the least concern him, did not even lift his eyebrows while it was being pronounced. Just as the clerk was calling the next case, he rose, and said, "I offer bail."

"You have that right," returned the judge.

Fix's blood ran cold, but he resumed his composure when he heard the judge announce that the bail required for each prisoner would be one thousand pounds.

"I will pay at once," said Mr Fogg, taking a roll of bank-bills from the carpet-bag, which Passepartout had by him, and placing them on the clerk's desk.

"This sum will be restored to you upon your release from prison," said the judge. "Meanwhile, you are liberated on bail."

"Come!" said Phileas Fogg to his servant.

Mr Fogg offered his arm to Aouda, then departed. Fix still nourished hopes that the robber would not, after all, leave the two thousand pounds behind him, but would decide to serve out his week in jail, and issued forth on Mr Fogg's traces. That gentleman took a carriage, and the party were soon landed on one of the quays.

The *Rangoon* was moored half a mile off in the harbour, its signal of departure at the mast-head. Eleven o'clock was striking; Mr Fogg was an hour in advance of time. Fix saw them leave the carriage and push off in a boat for the steamer, and stamped his feet with disappointment.

The Voyage to Hong Kong

The trip from Calcutta to Hong Kong comprised some three thousand five hundred miles, occupying from ten to twelve days.

During the first days of the journey, Aouda became better acquainted with her protector, and constantly gave evidence of her deep gratitude for what he had done. She also had a relative at Hong Kong whom she hoped to join.

Meanwhile, Fix was in hiding. He had managed to embark on the *Rangoon* at Calcutta without being seen by Passepartout, after leaving orders that, if the warrant should arrive, it should be forwarded to him at Hong Kong.

During the afternoon of Wednesday, October 30th, the *Rangoon* entered the Strait of Malacca, and weighed anchor at Singapore the next day at four a.m. to receive coal, having gained half a day on the prescribed times of her arrival.

At eleven o'clock the *Rangoon* rode out of Singapore harbour, and in a few hours the high mountains of Malacca were lost to view.

Singapore is distant some thirteen hundred miles from the island of Hong Kong. Phileas Fogg hoped to accomplish the journey in six days, so as to be in time for the steamer which would leave on the 6th of November for Yokohama, the principal Japanese port.

The weather, which had hitherto been fine, changed with the last quarter of the moon. The sea rolled heavily, and the wind at intervals rose almost to a storm. During the latter days of the voyage the weather worsened, the wind blew a gale and retarded the steamer. A sort of tempest arose on the 3rd November, the squall knocking the vessel about with fury and the waves running high. The steamer was forced to proceed slowly.

On the 4th November, however, the sea became more calm, and the storm lessened its violence; the wind veered southward, and was once more favourable. Some of the sails were unfurled, and the *Rangoon* resumed its most rapid speed.

The time lost could not, however, be regained. Land was not signalled until five o'clock on the morning of the 6th; Phileas Fogg was twenty-four hours behindhand, and the Yokohama steamer would, of course, be missed.

The pilot went on board at six, and took his place on the bridge, to guide the *Rangoon* through the channels to the port of Hong Kong.

Mr Fogg did not hesitate to approach the pilot and tranquilly ask him if he knew when a steamer would leave Hong Kong for Yokohama.

"At high tide tomorrow morning," answered the pilot.

"What's the steamer's name?" asked Mr Fogg.

"The *Carnatic*."

"Ought she not to have gone yesterday?"

"Yes, sir; but they had to repair one of her boilers, and so her departure was postponed till tomorrow."

"Thank you," returned Mr Fogg, descending mathematically to the saloon.

At one o'clock the *Rangoon* was at the quay, and the passengers were going ashore.

Chance had strangely favoured Phileas Fogg, for, had not the *Carnatic* been forced to lie over for repairing her boilers, she would have left on the 6th of November, and the passengers for Japan would have been obliged to await for a week the sailing of the next steamer. Mr Fogg was, it is true, twenty-four hours behind his time; but this could not seriously imperil the remainder of his tour.

The *Carnatic* was announced to leave Hong Kong at five the next morning. Mr Fogg had sixteen hours in which to attend to his business there, which was to deposit Aouda safely with her wealthy relative.

But, on enquiry, they learned that he had left China for Europe, probably Holland. It was then decided that Aouda should accompany Mr Fogg and Passepartout to Europe.

Passepartout Is Tricked by Fix

On reaching the quay where they were to embark on the *Carnatic*, Passepartout was astonished to find Fix walking up and down. The detective seemed very much disturbed and disappointed. He had, indeed, good reasons to inveigh against the bad luck which pursued him. The warrant had not come! It was certainly on the way, but as certainly it could not now reach Hong Kong for several days; and this being the last English territory on Mr Fogg's route, the robber would escape unless he could manage to detain him.

"Well, Monsieur Fix," said Passepartout, "have you decided to go with us as far as America?"

"Yes," returned Fix, through his set teeth.

"Good!" exclaimed Passepartout, laughing heartily.

They entered the steamer office and secured cabins for four persons. The clerk, as he gave them the tickets, informed them that, the repairs on the *Carnatic* having been completed, the steamer would leave that very evening, and not next morning, as had been announced.

"That will suit my master all the better," said Passepartout. "I will go and let him know."

Fix now decided to make a bold move; he resolved to tell Passepartout all. It seemed to be the only possible means of keeping Phileas Fogg several days longer at Hong Kong. He accordingly invited his companion into a tavern which caught his eye on the quay.

They ordered two bottles of port, to which the Frenchman did ample justice, whilst Fix observed him with close attention.

"I want to have a serious talk with you," said Fix.

Passepartout, at this, looked attentively at his companion. Fix's face seemed to have a singular expression.

"What is it that you have to say?"

Fix placed a hand upon Passepartout's arm, and, lowering his voice said, "Listen to me. I am a police detective, sent out here by the London office."

"You, a detective?"

"I will prove it. Here is my commission."

Passepartout was speechless with astonishment when Fix displayed this document, the genuineness of which could not be doubted.

"Listen. On the 28th of last September a robbery of fifty-five thousand pounds was committed at the Bank of England by a person whose description was fortunately secured. Here is the description; it answers exactly to that of Mr Phileas Fogg."

"What nonsense!" cried Passepartout, striking the table with his fist. "My master is the most honourable of men."

"How can you tell? You know scarcely anything about him. You went into his service the day he came away; and he came away on a foolish pretext, without trunks, and carrying a large amount in banknotes. And yet you are bold enough to assert that he is an honest man!"

"Yes, yes," repeated the poor fellow mechanically.

"Would you like to be arrested as his accomplice?"

Passepartout, overcome by what he had heard, held his head between his hands, and did not dare to look at the detective. Phileas Fogg, the saviour of Aouda, that brave and generous man, a robber! And yet how many presumptions there were against him! Passepartout essayed to reject the suspicions which forced themselves upon his mind; he did not wish to believe that his master was guilty.

"Well, what do you want of me?" said he, at last, with an effort.

"See here," replied Fix: "I have tracked Mr Fogg to this place, but as yet I have failed to receive the warrant of arrest for which I sent to London. You must help me to keep him here in Hong Kong—"

"I! But I—"

"I will share with you the two thousand pounds' reward offered by the Bank of England."

"Never!" replied Passepartout, who tried to rise, but fell back, exhausted in mind and body. "Mr Fix," he stammered; "even should what you say be true—if my master is really the robber you are seeking for—which I deny—I have been, am, in his service; I have seen his generosity and goodness; and I will never betray him—not for all the gold in the world. I come from a village where they don't eat that kind of bread!"

"You refuse?"

"I refuse."

"Consider that I've said nothing," said Fix, "and let us drink."

"Yes; let us drink!"

Passepartout felt himself yielding more and more to the effects of the liquor. Fix, seeing that he must at all hazards be separated from his master, wished

to overcome him entirely. Some pipes full of opium lay upon the table. Fix slipped one into Passepartout's hand. He took it, put it between his lips, lit it, drew several puffs, and his head, becoming heavy under the influence of the narcotic, fell upon the table.

"At last!" said Fix, seeing Passepartout unconscious. "Mr Fogg will not be informed of the *Carnatic's* departure; and, if he is, he will have to go without this cursed Frenchman!"

And, after paying his bill, Fix left the tavern.

Journey to Yokohama

When Passepartout did not appear the next morning to answer his master's bell, Mr Fogg, not betraying the least vexation, contented himself with taking his carpet-bag, calling Aouda and sending for a palanquin.

It was then eight o'clock; at half-past nine, it being then high tide, the *Carnatic* would leave the harbour. Mr Fogg and Aouda got into the palanquin, their luggage being brought after on a

wheelbarrow, and half-an-hour later stepped upon the quay whence they were to embark. Mr Fogg then learned that the *Carnatic* had sailed the evening before. He had expected to find not only the steamer but his domestic, and was forced to give up both; but no sign of disappointment appeared on his face, and he merely remarked to Aouda, "It is an accident, madam; nothing more."

At this moment a man who had been observing him attentively approached. It was Fix, who, bowing, addressed Mr Fogg: "Were you not, like me, sir, a passenger by the *Rangoon*, which arrived yesterday?"

"I was sir," replied Mr Fogg coldly. "But I have not the honour—"

"Pardon me; I thought I should find your servant here."

"Do you know where he is, sir?" asked Aouda anxiously.

"What?" responded Fix, feigning surprise. "Is he not with you?"

"No," said Aouda. "He has not made his appearance since yesterday. Could he have gone on board the *Carnatic* without us?"

"Without you, madam?" answered the detective. "Excuse me, did you intend to sail in the *Carnatic*?"

"Yes sir."

"So did I, madam, and I am excessively disappointed. The *Carnatic*, its repairs being completed, left Hong Kong twelve hours before the stated time, without any notice being given; and we must now wait a week for another steamer."

As he said 'a week' Fix felt his heart leap for joy. Fogg retained at Hong Kong a week! There would be time for the warrant to arrive, and fortune at last favoured the representative of the law. His horror may be imagined when he heard Mr Fogg say, in his placid voice, "But there are other vessels besides the *Carnatic*, it seems to me, in the harbour of Hong Kong."

And, offering his arm to Aouda, he directed his steps towards the docks in search of some craft about to start. Fix, stupefied, followed. For three hours Phileas Fogg had wandered about the docks, when at length he was accosted by a sailor.

"Is your honour looking for a boat?"

"Have you a boat ready to sail?"

"Yes, your honour; a pilot-boat—No. 43—the best in the harbour."

"Does she go fast?"

"Between eight and nine knots an hour. Will you look at her?"

"Yes."

"Your honour will be satisfied with her. Is it for a sea excursion?"

"No; for a voyage."

"A voyage?"

"Yes; will you agree to take me to Yokohama? I have missed the *Carnatic*, and I must get to Yokohama by the 14th at the latest, to make the boat for San Francisco. I offer you a hundred pounds per day, and an additional reward of two hundred pounds if I reach Yokohama in time."

"Well, your honour," replied he, "I could not risk myself, my men, or my little boat of scarcely twenty tons on so long a voyage at this time of year. Besides, we could not reach Yokohama in time, for it is sixteen hundred and sixty miles from Hong Kong. But, it might be arranged another way,—by going to Shanghai, which is only eight hundred miles from here, and picking up the San Francisco steamer there, which is where it starts before putting in at Yokohama and Nagasaki."

"You are sure of that?"

"Perfectly."

"And when does the boat leave Shanghai?"

"On the 11th, at seven in the evening. We have, therefore, four days before us, that is ninety-six hours; and in that time, if we had good luck and a south-west wind, and the sea was calm, we could make those eight hundred miles to Shanghai."

"And could you go—?"

"In an hour; as soon as provisions could be got aboard and the sails put up."

"It is a bargain. Are you the master of the boat?"

"Yes; John Bunsby, master of the *Tankadere*."

"Here are two hundred pounds on account, sir," added Phileas Fogg, turning to Fix, "if you would like to take the advantage—"

"Thanks, sir; I was about to ask the favour."

"Very well. In half-an-hour we shall go on aboard."

While Fix, in a feverish, nervous state, repaired to the pilot-boat the others directed their course to the police-station at Hong Kong. Phileas Fogg there gave Passepartout's description and left a sum of money to be spent in the search for him.

Mr Fogg and Aouda then stopped at the hotel for the luggage, and returned to the wharf. It was now three o'clock; and pilot-boat No. 43, with its crew on board and its provisions stored away, was ready for departure.

The sails and the English flag were hoisted at ten minutes past three. Mr Fogg and Aouda, who were seated on deck, cast a last glance at the quay.

Knowing the Frenchman's pertinacity, and having had ample evidence of his faithful service, they had not given up all hope of his return. But Passepartout did not appear.

John Bunsby, master, at length gave the order to start, and the *Tankadere*, taking the wind under her brigantine, foresail, and standing-jib bounded briskly forward over the waves.

A Storm off Shanghai

At sunrise the next day, which was November 8th, the boat had made more than one hundred miles, and by evening, the log showed that two hundred and twenty miles had been accomplished from Hong Kong.

At daybreak the wind began to blow hard and the heavens seemed to predict a gale.

The night was really terrible; at times it was a miracle that the craft did not founder. Twice it would have been all over with her if the crew had not been constantly on the watch. Aouda was exhausted, but did not utter a complaint. More than once Mr Fogg rushed to protect her from the violence of the waves.

Day reappeared. The tempest still raged with undiminished fury; but the wind now returned to the

south-west and it was a favourable change, and the *Tankadere* again bounded forward on this mountainous sea.

There were some signs of a calm at noon, and these became more distinct as the sun descended toward the horizon. The tempest had been as brief as terrific.

The night was comparatively quiet. Some of the sails were again hoisted, and the speed of the boat was very good. At dawn they espied the coast.

John Bunsby found himself at six o'clock not more than ten miles from the mouth of Shanghai River. Shanghai itself is situated at least twelve miles up the stream. At seven they were still three miles from Shanghai. At this moment, a long, black funnel, crowned with wreaths of smoke, appeared on the edge of the waters. It was the American steamer, leaving for Yokohama at the appointed time.

"Signal her!" said Phileas Fogg quietly. "Hoist your flag!"

The flag was run up at half-mast, and, this being the signal of distress, it was hoped that the American steamer, perceiving it, would change her course a little, so as to succour the pilot-boat.

"Fire!" said Mr Fogg. And the booming of the little cannon resounded in the air.

Passepartout Arrives in Yokohama

Meanwhile, the *Carnatic*, setting sail from Hong Kong at half-past six on the 7th of November, directed her course at full steam towards Japan.

The next day a passenger with a half-stupefied eye, staggering gait, and disordered hair, was seen to emerge from the second cabin, and to totter to a seat on deck. It was Passepartout and what had happened to him was as follows.

Shortly after Fix had left, the poor fellow awoke, and struggled against the stupefying influence of the narcotic. Staggering and holding himself up by keeping against the walls, falling down and creeping up again, and irresistibly impelled by a kind of instinct, he kept crying out, "The *Carnatic!* The *Carnatic!*

The steamer lay puffing alongside the quay, on the point of starting. Passepartout had but a few steps to go; and, rushing upon the plank, he crossed it, and fell unconscious on the deck, just as the *Carnatic* was moving off. Several sailors, who were evidently accustomed to this sort of scene, carried the poor Frenchman down into the second cabin, and Passepartout did not wake until they were one hundred and fifty miles away from China.

He then realized that his master and Aouda were not on the steamer and remembered that the time of sailing had been changed, that he should have informed his master of that fact, and that he had not done so. It was his fault, then, that Mr Fogg and Aouda had missed the steamer, but it was still more the fault of the traitor who, in order to separate him from his master and retain the latter at Hong Kong, had inveigled him into getting drunk! He now saw the detective's trick. If Fix ever came within his reach, what a settling of accounts there would be!

After his first depression, Passepartout became calmer and began to study his situation. His passage

had fortunately been paid for in advance; and he had
five or six days in which to decide upon his future
course.

At dawn on the 13th the *Carnatic* entered the port
of Yokohama. Passepartout went timidly ashore. He
had nothing better to do than, taking chance for his
guide, to wander aimlessly through the streets of
Yokohama.

Night came, and Passepartout wandered through
the streets, lit by vari-coloured lanterns, looking on
at the dancers. Then he came to the harbour, which
was lit up by the rosin torches of the fishermen, who
were fishing from their boats.

Passepartout Is Reunited with His Master

What happened when the pilot-boat came in sight of Shanghai will be easily guessed. The signals made by the *Tankadere* had been seen by the captain of the Yokohama steamer, who, espying the flag at half-mast, had directed his course towards the little craft. Phileas Fogg, after paying the stipulated price of his passage to John Bunsby, and rewarding that worthy with the additional sum of five hundred and fifty pounds, ascended the steamer with Aouda and Fix; and they started at once for Nagasaki and Yokohama.

They reached their destination on the morning of the 14th of November. Phileas Fogg lost no time in going on board the *Carnatic* where he learned, to Aouda's great delight—and perhaps to his own, though he betrayed no emotion—that Passepartout, a Frenchman, had really arrived on her the day before.

The San Francisco steamer was announced to leave that very evening, and it became necessary to find Passepartout, if possible, without delay. And they did find him. Poor Passepartout was wandering along towards them, looking sad and jaded, until he looked up and saw his master.

"Ah, my master! my master!" he cried.

"Come on, young man!" said Mr Fogg encouragingly, "let us all go to the steamer."

Passepartout thought that the time had not yet arrived to divulge to his master what had taken place between the detective and himself; and in the account he gave of his absence he simply excused himself for having been overtaken by drunkenness in smoking opium at a tavern in Hong Kong.

At half-past six, the very hour of departure, Mr Fogg and Aouda, followed by Passepartout, looking very sorry for himself, stepped upon the American steamer.

Arrival in San Francisco

The steamer making its way to San Francisco belonged to the Pacific Mail Steamship Company, and was named the *General Grant*. She was a large paddle-wheel steamer of two thousand five hundred tons, well equipped and fast.

By making twelve miles an hour, she would cross the ocean in twenty-one days. Phileas Fogg was therefore justified in hoping that he would reach San Francisco by the 2nd of December, New York by the 11th, and London on the 20th—thus gaining several hours on the fatal date of the 21st of December.

A railway train from San Francisco to New York, and a transatlantic steamer from New York to Liverpool would doubtless bringing them to the end of this impossible journey round the world within the period agreed upon.

But where was Fix at this moment?

He was actually on board the *General Grant*. He had found the warrant at Yokohama and had not been able to see Mr Fogg that day, and now the warrant was useless, as Mr Fogg had left English ground. He therefore decided to follow Fogg to England and even to try, if he could, to hasten the journey.

On that very day, however, he met Passepartout face to face on the forward deck. The latter, without a word, made a rush for him, grasped him by the throat, and administered to the detective a perfect volley of blows, which proved the great superiority of French over English pugilistic skill.

When Passepartout had finished, he found himself relieved and comforted. Fix got up in a somewhat rumpled condition, and looking at his adversary, coldly said, "Have you done?"

"For the time—yes."

"Then let me have a word with you, in your master's interest."

Passepartout seemed to be vanquished by Fix's coolness, for he quietly followed him, and they sat down aside from the rest of the passengers.

"You have given me a thrashing," said Fix. "Good; I expected it. Now, Mr Fogg seems to be going back to England. Well, I will follow him there. But hereafter I will do as much to keep obstacles out of his way as I have done up to this time to put them in his path. I've changed my game, you see, and simply because it was for my interest to change it. Your interest is the same as mine; for it is only in England that you will ascertain whether you are in the service of a criminal or an honest man."

Passepartout listened very attentively to Fix, and was convinced that he spoke with entire good faith.

"Are we friends?" asked the detective.

"Friends?—no," replied Passepartout; "but allies, perhaps. At the least sign of treason, however, I'll twist your neck for you."

"Agreed," said the detective quietly.

Eleven days later, on the 3rd of December, the *General Grant* entered the bay of the Golden Gate, and reached San Francisco.

Mr Fogg had neither gained nor lost a single day.

An Encounter with Buffalo

Mr Fogg, on reaching shore, proceeded to find out at what hour the first train left for New York, and learned that this was at six o'clock p.m.; he had, therefore, an entire day to spend in the Californian capital.

He had not proceeded two hundred steps, however, when, by the greatest chance in the world, he met Fix. The detective seemed wholly taken by surprise. What! Had Mr Fogg and himself crossed the Pacific together, and not met on the steamer? At last Fix felt honoured to behold once more the gentleman to whom he owed so much, and as his business recalled him to Europe, he should be delighted to continue the journey in such pleasant company.

Mr Fogg replied that the honour would be his.

At a quarter before six the travellers reached the station, and found the train ready to depart. They all got into the train, which started off at full speed.

The railroad was to be traversed in seven days, which would enable Phileas Fogg—at least, so he hoped—to take the Atlantic steamer at New York on the 11th for Liverpool.

The travellers were asleep when they passed through Sacramento and later the train entered the range of the Sierra Nevada. San Francisco was reached at seven in the morning; then they entered and passed through the State of Nevada through the Carson Valley and reached Reno at midday, where there was a delay of twenty minutes for breakfast. They then proceeded through prairies, the mountains lining the horizon, and in the distance great herds of buffaloes, massing together, seemed like a moveable dam.

About twelve o'clock a troop of ten or twelve thousand head of buffalo encumbered the track. The locomotive, slackening its speed, tried to clear the way with its cow-catcher; but the mass of animals was too great. The buffaloes marched along with a tranquil gait, uttering now and then deafening bellowings. There was no use in interrupting them, for, having taken a particular direction, nothing can moderate and change their course; it is a torrent of living flesh which no dam could contain.

Passepartout was furious at the delay they occasioned.

The best course was to wait patiently, and regain the lost time by greater speed when the obstacle was removed.

When the track was clear, the train continued its immense journey across this vast country.

The train stopped at the Great Salt Lake, which Mr Fogg and his party were able to spend some time visiting, then sped on through Wyoming territory, over the Rocky Mountains and through limitless plains and prairies, some of which were infested with Indians, who frequently made furious attacks upon the train.

An Indian Attack

There was an occasion when Passepartout showed immense bravery when the train was under a particularly savage assault.

The train had left the important town of North Platte, and had passed Plum Creek, and was pursuing its course when suddenly, savage yells resounded in the air. Cries of terror proceeded from the interior of the cars as the occupants perceived that the train was being attacked by a band of Sioux.

This was not the first attempt of these daring Indians, for more than once they had waylaid trains on the road. A hundred of them had, according to their habit, jumped upon the steps without stopping the train, with the ease of a clown mounting a horse at full gallop.

The Sioux were armed with guns, from which came the reports, to which the passengers, who were almost all armed, responded by revolver-shots.

The Indians had first mounted the engine, and half stunned the engineer and stoker with blows from their muskets. A Sioux chief, wishing to stop the train, but not knowing how to work the regulator, had opened wide instead of closing the steam-valve, and the locomotive was plunging forward with terrific velocity.

The Sioux had at the same time invaded the cars, skipping like enraged monkeys over the roofs, thrusting open the doors, and fighting hand to hand with the passengers. Penetrating the baggage-room, they pillaged it, throwing the trunks out of the train.

The travellers defended themselves bravely; some of the cars were barricaded, and sustained a siege, like moving forts, carried along at a speed of a hundred miles an hour.

Aouda behaved courageously from the first. She defended herself like a true heroine with a revolver, which she shot through the broken windows whenever a savage made his appearance. Twenty Sioux had fallen mortally wounded to the ground, and the wheels crushed those who fell upon the rails as if they had been worms. Several passengers, shot or stunned, lay on the seats.

It was necessary to put an end to the struggle, which had lasted for ten minutes, and which would

result in the triumph of the Sioux if the train was not stopped. Fort Kearney station, where there was a garrison, was only two miles distant; but, that once passed, the Sioux would be masters of the train between Fort Kearney and the station beyond.

The conductor was fighting beside Mr Fogg, when he was shot and fell. At the same moment he cried, "Unless the train is stopped in five minutes, we are lost!"

"It shall be stopped," said Phileas Fogg, preparing to rush from the car.

"Stay, monsieur," cried Passepartout; "I will go."

Mr Fogg had not time to stop the brave fellow, who, opening a door unperceived by the Indians, succeeded in slipping under the car; and while the struggle continued, and the balls whizzed across each other over his head, he worked his way under the cars with amazing agility, holding on to the chains, aiding himself by the brakes and edges of the sashes, creeping from one car to another with marvellous skill, and thus gaining the forward end of the train.

There, suspended by one hand between the baggage-car and the tender, with the other he loosened the safety-chains; but, owing to the traction, he would never have succeeded in unscrewing the yoking-bar, had not a violent concussion jolted this bar out. The train, now detached from the engine, remained a little behind, whilst the locomotive rushed forward with increased speed with Passepartout on board!

Carried on by the force already acquired, the train still moved for several minutes; but the brakes were worked, and at last they stopped, less than a hundred feet from Kearney station.

The soldiers of the fort, attracted by the shots, hurried up; the Sioux had not expected them, and decamped in a body before the train entirely stopped.

Passepartout had at last revived the engineer and together they brought the locomotive to a standstill before returning to join the passenger cars.

There were many wounded, but none mortally. All the passengers got out of the train, the wheels of which were stained with blood. From the tyres and spokes hung ragged pieces of flesh. As far as the eye could reach on the white plains behind, red trails were visible. The last Sioux were disappearing in the south, along the banks of the Republican River.

Everyone was safe—they were all saved through the devotion of the courageous Frenchman.

A Night in New York

The train now passed rapidly across the State of Iowa, by Council Bluffs, Des Moines, and Iowa City. During the night it crossed the Mississippi at Davenport, and by Rock Island entered Illinois. The next day, which was the 10th, at four in the evening, it reached Chicago, already risen from its ruins, and more proudly seated than ever on the borders of its beautiful Lake Michigan.

Nine hundred miles separated Chicago from New York; but trains are not wanting at Chicago. Mr Fogg passed at once from one to the other, and the locomotive of the Pittsburg, Fort Wayne and Chicago Railway left at full speed, as if it fully comprehended that that gentleman had no time to lose. It traversed Indiana, Ohio, Pennsylvania, and New Jersey like a flash, rushing through towns with antique names, some of which had streets and car-tracks, but as yet no houses. At last the Hudson came into view; and at a quarter-past eleven in the evening of the 11th, the train stopped in the station on the right bank of the river, before the very pier of the Cunard line.

The *China*, for Liverpool, had started three-quarters of an hour before!

The *China*, in leaving, seemed to have carried off Phileas Fogg's last hope.

"We will consult about what is best tomorrow. Come," he said coolly.

The party crossed the Hudson in the Jersey City ferryboat, and drove in a carriage to the St. Nicholas Hotel, on Broadway. Rooms were engaged, and the night passed, briefly to Phileas Fogg, who slept profoundly, but very long to Aouda and the others, whose agitation did not permit them to rest.

The next day was the 12th of December. Mr Fogg left the hotel alone, after giving Passepartout instructions to await his return, and inform Aouda to be ready at an instant's notice. He proceeded to the banks of the Hudson, and looked about among the vessels moored or anchored in the river for any that were about to depart.

He seemed about to give up all hope, when he espied, anchored at the Battery, a cable's length off at most, a trading vessel, with a screw, well-shaped, whose funnel, puffing a cloud of smoke, indicated that she was getting ready for departure.

This was the *Henrietta*, bound for Bordeaux.

Mr Fogg was only able to secure his passage for an enormous sum of money, as the Captain was travelling with freight and had no need for passengers. The Captain was offered two thousand dollars apiece for himself and the crew, which totalled eight thousand dollars!

When Passepartout heard what this last voyage was going to cost, he uttered a prolonged "Oh!" which extended throughout his vocal gamut.

As for Fix, he said to himself that the Bank of England would certainly not come out of this affair well indemnified. When they reached England, even if Mr Fogg did not throw some handfuls of bank-bills into the sea, more than seven thousand pounds would have been spent.

Mr Fogg and his party were all on board, when the *Henrietta* made ready to weigh anchor at nine o'clock.

Phileas Fogg Takes Command

At noon the next day a man mounted the bridge to ascertain the vessel's position. It may be thought that this was the captain of the *Henrietta*. Not the least in the world. It was Phileas Fogg, Esquire. As for the captain, Captain Speedy, he was shut up in his cabin under lock and key, and was uttering loud cries, which signified an anger at once pardonable and excessive.

What had happened was very simple. Phileas Fogg wished to go to Liverpool, but the captain would not carry him there. Then Phileas Fogg, during the thirty hours he had been on board, had so shrewdly managed with his banknotes that the sailors and stokers, who were an occasional crew, and were not on the best of terms with the captain, went over to him in a body. This was why Phileas Fogg was in command instead of Captain Speedy. The *Henrietta* was directing her course towards Liverpool. It was very clear, to see Mr Fogg manage the craft, that he had been a sailor. As for Passepartout, he thought Mr Fogg's manoeuvre simply glorious.

On the 13th they passed the edge of the Banks of Newfoundland, a dangerous locality; ever since the evening before, the barometer, suddenly falling, had indicated an approaching change in the atmosphere; and during the night the temperature varied, the cold became sharper, and the wind veered to the south-east. This was a misfortune. Mr Fogg, in order not to deviate from his course, furled his sails and increased the force of the steam; the vessel's speed slackened. But Phileas Fogg was a bold mariner, and knew how to maintain headway against the sea; and he kept on his course, without even decreasing his steam.

The 16th of December was the seventy-fifth day since Phileas Fogg's departure from London, and the *Henrietta* had not yet been seriously delayed. Half of the voyage was almost accomplished.

But on this day the engineer came on deck, went up to Mr Fogg and began to speak earnestly with him—they were running out of coal! And on the 18th, the engineer, as he had predicted, announced that the coal would give out during the course of the day.

"Do not on any account let the fires go down," said Mr Fogg. "Keep them up to the last. Let the valves be filled."

Towards noon Phileas Fogg, having ascertained their position, called Passepartout, and ordered him to go for Captain Speedy. It was as if the honest fellow had been commanded to unchain a tiger. He went to the poop, saying to himself, "He will be like a madman!"

In a few moments, with cries and oaths, a bomb appeared on the poop-deck. The bomb was Captain Speedy. It was clear that he was on the point of bursting.

"Where are we?" were the first words his anger permitted him to utter.

"Seven hundred and seven miles from Liverpool," replied Mr Fogg, with imperturbable calmness.

"Pirate!" cried Captain Speedy.

"I have sent for you, sir," continued Mr Fogg, "to ask you to sell me your vessel."

"No! By all the devils, no!"

"But I shall be obliged to burn her."

"Burn the *Henrietta!* Burn my vessel!" cried Captain Speedy, "a vessel worth fifty thousand dollars!"

"Here are sixty thousand," replied Phileas Fogg, handing the captain a roll of bank-bills.

This had a prodigious effect on Andrew Speedy. An American can scarcely remain unmoved at the sight of sixty thousand dollars. The captain forgot in an instant his anger, his imprisonment, and all his grudges against his passenger. The *Henrietta* was twenty years old; it was a great bargain. The bomb would not go off, after all.

"Agreed," said Captain Speedy.

During this colloquy, Passepartout was as white as a sheet, and Fix seemed on the point of having an apoplectic fit. Nearly twenty thousand pounds had been expended. It was true, however, that fifty-five thousand pounds had been stolen from the bank.

Then Mr Fogg gave orders to have the interior seats, bunks, and frames pulled down, and burnt. It was necessary to have dry wood to keep the steam up to the adequate pressure, and on that day the poop, cabins, bunks, and the spare deck were sacrificed. On the next day, the 19th of December, the masts, rafts, and spars were burned. The railings, fittings, the greater part of the deck, and top sides, disappeared on the 20th. But on this day they sighted the Irish coast and Fastnet Light, and by ten in the evening they were passing Queenstown; and the steam was about to give out altogether!

Queenstown is the Irish port at which the transatlantic steamers stop to put off the mails. These mails are carried to Dublin by express trains always held in readiness to start; from Dublin they are sent on to Liverpool by the most rapid boats, and thus gain twelve hours on the Atlantic steamers.

Phileas Fogg counted on gaining twelve hours in the same way. The *Henrietta* entered Queenstown Harbour at one o'clock in the morning.

Phileas Fogg at last disembarked on the Liverpool quay, at twenty minutes before twelve, December 21st. He was only six hours distant from London.

But at this moment Fix came up, put his hand upon Mr Fogg's shoulder, and, showing his warrant, said, "You are really Phileas Fogg?"

"I am."

"I arrest you in the Queen's name!"

No Time to Lose

Phileas Fogg was in prison. He had been shut up in the Custom House, and he was to be transferred to London the next day.

If anyone, at this moment, had entered the Custom House, he would have found Mr Fogg seated, motionless, calm, and without apparent anger, upon a wooden bench. He was not, it is true, resigned; but this last blow failed to force him into an outward betrayal of any emotion.

The Custom House clock struck one. Mr Fogg observed that his watch was two hours too fast.

Two hours! Admitting that he was at this moment taking an express train, he could reach London and the Reform Club by a quarter before nine, p.m. His forehead slightly wrinkled.

At thirty-three minutes past two he heard a singular noise outside, then a hasty opening of doors. Passepartout's voice was audible, and immediately after, that of Fix. Phileas Fogg's eyes brightened for an instant.

The door swung open, and he saw Passepartout, Aouda, and Fix, who hurried towards him.

Fix was out of breath, and his hair was in disorder. He could not speak. "Sir," he stammered, "sir—forgive me—a most—unfortunate resemblance—robber arrested three days ago—you—are free!"

Phileas Fogg was free! He walked to the detective, looked him steadily in the face, and with the only rapid motion he had ever made in his life, or which he ever would make, drew back his arm, and with the precision of a machine, knocked Fix down.

Mr Fogg, Aouda, and Passepartout left the Custom House without delay, got into a cab, and in a few moments descended at the station.

Phileas Fogg asked if there was an express train about to leave for London. It was forty minutes past two. The express train had already left. Phileas Fogg then ordered a special train. There were several rapid locomotives on hand; but the railway arrangements did not permit the special train to leave until three o'clock.

At that hour, Phileas Fogg, having stimulated the engineer by the offer of a generous reward, at last set out towards London with Aouda and his faithful servant.

Unfortunately there were forced delays, and when Mr Fogg stepped from the train at the terminus, clocks in London were striking ten minutes before nine.

Having made the tour of the world, he was behindhand five minutes. He had lost the wager!

Defeat

Mr Fogg bore his misfortune with his habitual tranquility. Mr Fogg's course, however, was fully decided upon; he knew what remained for him to do.

A room in the house in Savile Row was set apart for Aouda, who was overwhelmed with grief at her protector's misfortune.

Knowing that Englishmen governed by a fixed idea sometimes resort to the desperate expedient of suicide, Passepartout kept a narrow watch upon his master, though he carefully concealed the appearance of so doing.

The night passed. Mr Fogg went to bed. Aouda did not once close her eyes. Passepartout watched all night, like a faithful dog, at his master's door.

The next day Mr Fogg had no reason for going out, and so he remained at home. He shut himself up in his room, and busied himself putting his affairs in order.

About half-past seven in the evening Mr Fogg sent to know if Aouda would receive him, and in a few moments he found himself alone with her.

Later Passepartout was summoned and appeared immediately. Mr Fogg still held Aouda's hand in his own; Passepartout understood, and his big, round face became as radiant as the tropical sun at its zenith. Phileas Fogg and Aouda had decided to be married!

Mr Fogg asked Passepartout if it was not too late to notify the Reverend Samuel Wilson, of Marylebone parish, that evening.

Passepartout smiled his most genial smile, and said, "Never too late."

It was five minutes past eight.

"Will it be for tomorrow, Monday?"

"For tomorrow, Monday," said Mr Fogg, turning to Aouda.

"Yes; for tomorrow, Monday," she replied.

Passepartout hurried off as fast as his legs could carry him.

The Wager Is Won

On Saturday, the 21st December in the evening, the five antagonists of Phileas Fogg had met in the great saloon of the club. They were in a state of feverish suspense. Would Phileas Fogg reappear before their eyes?

The clock indicated eighteen minutes to nine.

The players took up their cards, but could not keep their eyes off the clock. Certainly, however secure they felt, minutes had never seemed so long to them!

"Seventeen minutes to nine," said Thomas Flanagan, as he cut the cards which Ralph handed to him.

Then there was a moment of silence. The great saloon was perfectly quiet.

"Sixteen minutes to nine!" said John Sullivan, in a voice which betrayed his emotion.

One minute more, and the wager would be won. Andrew Stuart and his partners suspended their game. They left their cards, and counted the seconds.

At the fortieth second, nothing. At the fiftieth, still nothing.

At the fifty-fifth, a loud cry was heard in the street.

The players rose from their seats.

At the fifty-seventh second the door of the saloon opened; and the pendulum had not beat the sixtieth second when Phileas Fogg appeared, followed by an excited crowd who had forced their way through the club doors, and in a calm voice, said, "Here I am, gentlemen!"

Yes; Phileas Fogg in person!

The reader will remember that at five minutes past eight in the evening—about four and twenty hours after the arrival of the travellers in London—Passepartout had been sent by his master to engage the services of the Reverend Samuel Wilson in a certain marriage ceremony, which was to take place the next day.

In thirty minutes Passepartout had returned to Savile Row again, and staggered breathlessly into Mr Fogg's room.

He could not speak.

"What is the matter?" asked Mr Fogg.

"My master," gasped Passepartout, "marriage—impossible, because tomorrow—is Sunday!"

"Monday," replied Mr Fogg.

"No—today—is Saturday."

"Saturday? Impossible!"

"Yes, yes, yes, yes," cried Passepartout. "You have made a mistake of one day! We arrived twenty–four hours ahead of time; but there are only ten minutes left!"

Passepartout had seized his master by the collar, and was dragging him along with irresistible force.

Phileas Fogg, thus kidnapped, without having time to think, left his house, jumped into a cab, promised a hundred pounds to the cabman, and finally reached the Reform Club.

The clock indicated a quarter before nine when he appeared in the great saloon.

Phileas Fogg had accomplished the journey round the world in eighty days.

The cause of the error is very simple.

Phileas Fogg had, without suspecting it, gained one day on his journey, and this merely because he had travelled constantly *eastward*; he would, on the contrary, have lost a day had he gone in the opposite direction, that is, *westward*.

In journeying eastward he had gone towards the sun, and the days therefore diminished for him as many times four minutes as he crossed degrees in this direction. There are three hundred and sixty degrees on the circumference of the earth; and these three hundred and sixty degrees, multiplied by four minutes, give precisely twenty-four hours – that is, the day unconsciously gained. In other words, while Phileas Fogg, going eastward, saw the sun pass the meridian *eighty* times, his friends in London only saw it pass the meridian *seventy-nine* times. This is why they awaited him at the Reform Club on Saturday, and not Sunday, as Mr Fogg thought.

Phileas Fogg, then, had won the twenty thousand pounds; but as he had spent nearly nineteen thousand on the way, the pecuniary gain was small. His object was, however, to be victorious, and not to win money. He divided the one thousand pounds that remained between Passepartout and the unfortunate Fix, against whom he cherished no grudge.

It need not be said that the marriage took place forty-eight hours after, and that Passepartout, glowing and dazzling, gave the bride away. Had he not saved her, and was he not entitled to this honour?

The next day, as soon as it was light, Passepartout rapped vigorously at his master's door. Mr Fogg opened it, and asked, "What's the matter, Passepartout?"

"What is it, sir? Why, I've just this instant found out——"

"What?"

"That we might have made the tour of the world in only seventy-eight days."

"No doubt," returned Mr Fogg, "by not crossing India. But if I had not crossed India, I should not have saved Aouda; she would not have been my wife, and—" Mr Fogg quietly shut the door.

Phileas Fogg had won his wager, and had made his journey around the world in eighty days.